# Dash to Dig

Written by Samantha Montgomerie
Illustrated by Dean Gray

## Collins

# Zip has the map.

Pel can dash.

3

Fuzz is quick.

Fuzz and Zip dig.

This box is big.

They chuck in the rings.

9

11

Pel cannot dash.

# We will not be rich!

/ch/

14

/nk/

# After reading

**Letters and Sounds:** Phase 3

**Word count:** 40

**Focus phonemes:** /w/ /x/ /z/ zz /qu/ /ch/ /sh/ /th/ /ng/ /nk/

**Common exception words:** and, to, the, we, they, be

**Curriculum links:** Personal, social and emotional development; Understanding the world

**Early learning goals:** Reading: read and understand simple sentences; use phonic knowledge to decode regular words and read them aloud accurately; read some common irregular words

## Developing fluency

- Your child may enjoy hearing you read the book.
- Ask your child to read the speech bubbles and sounds with expression, using a different tone for Fuzz and Pel.

## Phonic practice

- Reread page 4. Ask your child to find pairs of letters that together make one sound. (*F/u/zz, qu/i/ck*)
- Ask your child to sound out and blend the following:

  qu/i/ck   ch/u/ck   r/i/ng/s   d/a/sh   th/u/nk

- Say the words above and challenge your child to spell them out loud.
- Look at the "I spy sounds" pages (14 and 15) together. Take turns to find and say a word in the picture containing a /ch/ or /nk/ sound. (e.g. *chair, chess, beach, chest, chuck, cherry juice, chicks*; *drink, sinking ship, wink, pink*)

## Extending vocabulary

- Ask your child to suggest words with a similar meaning to these:

  dash (page 3)   thunk (page 6)   chuck (page 9)   quick (page 10)